Welcome To The World

Dear baby cousin,

You have so much ahead of you and are going to do great things. I know that you will be loved and protected every single second of your life.

You are going to be our ray of sunshine, and I know you will change the world.

Welcome to the World
Little one!
Love,
Madi ♡

On the day
you were born
everything
changed.

WELCOME TO
THE WORLD!

The World is very

big

with lots of wonderful places to visit.

YOU ARE LOVED

This is the beginning of
your amazing journey.

Your world is filled with beautiful things ...

tiny things ...

HUGE THINGS . . .

plants and flowers,
animals, birds
and insects

and so much COLOR.

Oceans and deserts,
mountains and forests...

laughter, love, wonder and joy.

As you grow,
make sure you
find time to chase
butterflies ...

and make a
SPLASH!

Dance in the summer rain....

and search for fairies.

May your wishes
be granted

and your skies filled with sunshine.

Remember that

things will change

and time will fly.

Trust in yourself and
reach for the stars.

The world is an exciting place, full of fun, adventure

and lots
and lots of
people.

There is only one

y o u

and to your
family and friends
YOU ARE
THEIR
WORLD!

Welcome To The World first published by FROM YOU TO ME LTD, in 2017.

For a full range of all our titles where gifts can also be personalised, please visit

WWW.FROMYOUTOME.COM

FROM YOU TO ME are committed to a sustainable future for our business, our customers and our planet. This book is printed and bound, in China, on FSC® certified paper.

Written and illustrated by Lucy Tapper & Steve Wilson fromlucy.com

9   11   13   15   14   12   10   8

Copyright © 2020 FROM YOU TO ME LTD

ISBN 978-1-907860-51-5

Available titles in the range: Welcome To The World & You're The Biggest